U0005078

新月集【全新插畫雙語版】

泰戈爾／著　　伍晴文／譯

The Crescent Moon

By Rabindranath Tagore

好讀出版

目 錄 Table of contents

我獨自漫步在穿過田野的小徑上，夕陽像個守財奴，正藏起它最後一塊金子。

白晝逐漸沒入更深沉的黑暗中，而那已收割的寂地，靜靜躺在那兒。

頃時間，有個男孩的高亢歌聲響入雲霄。他穿過看不見的黑幕，讓歌聲音韻迴盪在夜晚的寂靜中。

他村裡的家就坐落這塊荒地底端，甘蔗園後邊，隱藏在芭蕉、瘦長的檳榔樹、椰子樹和深綠色波羅蜜果樹影裡。

我在星空下的寂路上佇立了一會兒，看著暗沉的大地於我面前展開，用她的雙臂攬抱無數個家庭，那裡有搖籃和床，有母親的心和夜燈，還有滿心歡喜的年輕生命，渾然不知這歡樂對世界的價值。

THE HOME

I paced alone on the road across the field while the
sunset was hiding its last gold like a miser.

The daylight sank deeper and deeper into the
darkness, and the widowed land, whose harvest
had been reaped, lay silent.

Suddenly a boy's shrill voice rose into the sky. He
traversed the dark unseen, leaving the track of
his song across the hush of the evening.

His village home lay there at the end of the waste
land, beyond the sugar-cane field, hidden
among the shadows of the banana and the
slender areca palm, the cocoa-nut and the dark
green jack-fruit trees.

I stopped for a moment in my lonely way under
the starlight, and saw spread before me the
darkened earth surrounding with her arms
countless homes furnished with cradles and
beds, mothers' hearts and evening lamps, and
young lives glad with a gladness that knows
nothing of its value for the world.

海邊

孩子們在無垠世界的海邊相聚。

遼闊無邊的穹蒼凝止於頭頂，奔流不息的海水喧嚷不休。孩子們在無垠世界的海邊相聚，叫著、舞著。

他們拿沙造房子、拿空貝殼玩耍。他們拿落葉編織成船，笑著將之放入大海。孩子們在這世界的海邊嬉遊著。

他們不知如何游泳，也不知如何撒網。採珠人潛入海裡採珠，商人駛著他們的船航行，而孩子們只是撿拾起小石頭，又將之拋出。他們不去追尋寶藏，也不知如何撒網。

大海歡笑著捲起浪花，海灘的微笑閃耀著淡淡光芒。洶湧險惡的海浪對孩子們吟唱著無意義的歌曲，就像母親輕推著她孩子的搖籃那樣。大海陪孩子們玩耍，海灘的微笑閃耀著淡淡光芒。

孩子們在無垠世界的海邊相聚。狂風暴雨掃過無痕的天空，船隻沉碎在無痕的大海，死亡將近，而孩子們還在玩耍。孩子們在無垠世界的海邊，歡樂地齊聚一處。

02

ON THE SEASHORE

On the seashore of endless worlds children meet.

The infinite sky is motionless overhead and the restless water is boisterous. On the seashore of endless worlds the children meet with shouts and dances.

They build their houses with sand, and they play with empty shells. With withered leaves they weave their boats and smilingly float them on the vast deep. Children have their play on the seashore of worlds.

They know not how to swim, they know not how to cast nets. Pearl-fishers dive for pearls, merchants sail in their ships, while children gather pebbles and scatter them again. They seek not for hidden treasures, they know not how to cast nets.

The sea surges up with laughter, and pale gleams the smile of the sea-beach. Death-dealing waves sing meaningless ballads to the children, even like a mother while rocking her baby's cradle. The sea plays with children, and pale gleams the smile of the sea-beach.

On the seashore of endless worlds children meet. Tempest roams in the pathless sky, ships are wrecked in the trackless water, death is abroad and children play. On the seashore of endless worlds is the great meeting of children.

來源

掠過孩子雙眸的睡眠——有誰知道它來自何方？是的，據傳它棲息於森林蔭影中有螢火蟲微光照耀著的精靈村裡，那裡掛著兩片迷人的羞怯花蕾。它從那裡前來親吻孩子的雙眸。

孩子睡著時，浮現在他雙唇的那抹微笑——有誰知道它來自何方？是的，據傳新月那道新生的微光，觸及將逝的秋雲邊緣，那抹微笑便是誕生於這沐浴露珠的晨夢裡——孩子睡著時，浮現在他雙唇的那抹微笑。

孩子四肢所綻放那股芬芳又柔嫩的清新氣息——有誰知道它藏在哪裡藏了這麼久？是的，當母親還是少女時，它已潛伏在她心裡，在愛的溫柔與沉靜的神祕裡——孩子四肢所綻放那股芬芳又柔嫩的清新氣息。

THE SOURCE

The sleep that flits on baby's eyes — does anybody
   know from where it comes? Yes, there is a rumour
   that it has its dwelling where, in the fairy village
   among shadows of the forest dimly lit with glow-
   worms, there hang two shy buds of enchantment.
   From there it comes to kiss baby's eyes.

The smile that flickers on baby's lips when he sleeps
   — does anybody know where it was born? Yes,
   there is a rumour that a young pale beam of
   a crescent moon touched the edge of a vanishing
   autumn cloud, and there the smile was first born
   in the dream of a dew-washed morning — the
   smile that flickers on baby's lips when he sleeps.

The sweet, soft freshness that blooms on baby's limbs
   — does anybody know where it was hidden so
   long? Yes, when the mother was a young girl
   it lay pervading her heart in tender and silent
   mystery of love — the sweet, soft freshness that
   has bloomed on baby's limbs.

孩童之道

只要孩子願意，此刻便可飛上天堂。

他之所以不離開我們，並非毫無理由。

他喜歡將頭倚靠在母親懷中，半刻也不能看不見她。

孩子知道各種智慧之語，即使這世上極少人知曉其義。

他之所以從不想說話，並非毫無理由。

他想做的某一件事，便是學習從母親唇間吐出的話語。

這也是他看起來如此天真的原因。

孩子坐擁成堆的金銀珠寶，卻像個乞兒似的來到這世界。

他之所以透過如此偽裝來到這世界，並非毫無理由。

這可愛的小乞兒，裸著身體裝出一副全然無助的模樣，

這麼一來他便可以向母親乞求愛的財富。

BABY'S WAY

If baby only wanted to, he could fly up to heaven this moment.

It is not for nothing that he does not leave us.

He loves to rest his head on mother's bosom, and cannot ever bear
to lose sight of her.

Baby knows all manner of wise words, though few on earth can
understand their meaning.

It is not for nothing that he never wants to speak.

The one thing he wants is to learn mother's words from mother's
lips. That is why he looks so innocent.

Baby had a heap of gold and pearls, yet he came like a beggar on to
this earth.

It is not for nothing he came in such a disguise.

This dear little naked mendicant pretends to be utterly helpless,
so that he may beg for mother's wealth of love.

孩子在纖細的新月國度裡，自由自在、毫無拘束。

他之所以放棄自由，並非毫無理由。

他知道母親心窩有個小小的角落，藏著無窮無盡的歡樂，被母親愛的臂彎緊緊擁住，可遠比自由還要甜美。

孩子從不知如何哭泣。他住在極樂境邑裡。

他之所以選擇流淚，並非毫無理由。

雖然他可愛臉上的微笑，讓母親的心緊緊繫著他，但他因為小麻煩所發出的小小哭聲，卻織成了憐憫與關愛的雙重疼惜。

Baby was so free from every tie in the land of the tiny crescent moon.

It was not for nothing he gave up his freedom.

He knows that there is room for endless joy in mother's little corner of a heart, and it is sweeter far than liberty to be caught and pressed in her dear arms.

Baby never knew how to cry. He dwelt in the land of perfect bliss.

It is not for nothing he has chosen to shed tears.

Though with the smile of his dear face he draws mother's yearning heart to him, yet his little cries over tiny troubles weave the double bond of pity and love.

不受注意的盛典

啊，誰把那身小衣裳染上顏色的，我的孩子，誰在你那惹人喜愛的

四肢套上那件小紅衫？

你一早便跑到庭院玩耍，跑的時候跌跌又撞撞。

但究竟是誰把那身小衣裳染上顏色的，我的孩子？

什麼事逗你笑了，我生命的小花蕾？

母親站在門邊對你露出微笑。

她拍著手，腕上的鐲子叮噹作響，而你拿著竹竿手舞足蹈，活像個

小牧童。

但究竟是什麼事逗你笑了，我生命的小花蕾？

THE UNHEEDED PAGEANT

Ah, who was it coloured that little frock, my child, and covered your sweet limbs with that little red tunic?

You have come out in the morning to play in the courtyard, tottering and tumbling as you run.

But who was it coloured that little frock, my child?

What is it makes you laugh, my little life-bud?

Mother smiles at you standing on the threshold.

She claps her hands and her bracelets jingle, and you dance with your bamboo stick in your hand like a tiny little shepherd.

But what is it makes you laugh, my little life-bud?

喔，小乞兒，你雙手摟著媽媽的脖子想要乞求些什麼？

喔，貪婪的心兒，要我把整個世界從天上摘下來，像摘果實般放在你小小的紅嫩掌心上嗎？

喔，小乞兒，你想要乞求些什麼？

風歡歡喜喜地帶走了你踝鈴的叮噹聲。

太陽微笑地看著你梳洗。

當你在母親的臂彎裡睡著時，天空從上護望著你，早晨躡手躡腳來到你床前，親吻著你的雙眼。

風歡歡喜喜地帶走了你踝鈴的叮噹聲。

夢中精靈正穿過微明的天空，朝你飛來呢。

世界之母在你母親心中，保留了在你身旁的位置。

那個向群星演奏音樂的人，正拿著他的長笛站在你窗前。

夢中精靈正穿過微明的天空，朝你飛來呢。

O beggar, what do you beg for, clinging to your mother's neck with both your hands?

O greedy heart, shall I pluck the world like a fruit from the sky to place it on your little rosy palm?

O beggar, what are you begging for?

The wind carries away in glee the tinkling of your anklet bells.

The sun smiles and watches your toilet.

The sky watches over you when you sleep in your mother's arms, and the morning comes tiptoe to your bed and kisses your eyes.

The wind carries away in glee the tinkling of your anklet bells.

The fairy mistress of dreams is coming towards you, flying through the twilight sky.

The world-mother keeps her seat by you in your mother's heart.

He who plays his music to the stars is standing at your window with his flute.

And the fairy mistress of dreams is coming towards you, flying through the twilight sky.

竊眠者

誰從孩子的雙眸偷走了睡眠？我一定得知道。

母親將水罐挾在腰間，到附近村莊汲水。

那是正午時分，孩子玩耍的時間已經過了，池塘裡的鴨子寂靜無聲。

牧童躺在榕樹蔭影下睡著了。

白鶴沉靜地站在芒果園旁的沼澤中。

就在此時，竊眠者過來從孩子的雙眸偷走睡眠，飛走了。

當母親回來時，發現孩子四肢著地在屋裡爬著。

是誰從孩子的雙眸偷走了睡眠？我一定得知道。我得找到她並綁住她。

我得到黑洞那兒找找，洞裡的水滴淌過圓卵石和沉石，匯聚成一泓小溪流。

我一定得到醉花叢那沉寂的蔭影處找找，鴿子在牠們棲息的角落咕咕叫著，精靈的腳環叮噹響徹滿天星斗的寂靜夜空。

SLEEP-STEALER

Who stole sleep from baby's eyes? I must know.

Clasping her pitcher to her waist, mother went to fetch water from the village near by.

It was noon. The children's playtime was over; the ducks in the pond were silent.

The shepherd boy lay asleep under the shadow of the *banyan* tree.

The crane stood grave and still in the swamp near the mango grove.

In the meanwhile the Sleep-stealer came and, snatching sleep from baby's eyes, flew away.

When mother came back she found baby travelling the room over on all fours.

Who stole sleep from our baby's eyes? I must know. I must find her and chain her up.

I must look into that dark cave, where, through boulders and scowling stones, trickles a tiny stream.

I must search in the drowsy shade of the *bakula* grove, where pigeons coo in their corner, and fairies' anklets tinkle in the stillness of starry nights.

入夜後，我會到寂語喃喃的竹林窺看。螢火蟲在那裡揮霍牠們的光芒，我會向我遇見的每一個生物問：「有誰能告訴我竊眠者住在哪裡嗎？」

誰從孩子的雙眸偷走了睡眠？我一定得知道。

假如我能抓到她，肯定要好好教訓她！

我要闖入她的老巢，看看她把所有偷來的睡眠都藏到哪兒去了。

我要將之全部奪回。

我會將她的兩翼牢牢縛住，將她放在河岸邊，讓她在燈心草與睡蓮間拿著一根蘆葦乖乖玩釣魚遊戲。

當市場於晚間收市後，村裡的孩子坐在母親膝上時，夜鳥將來到她耳邊嘲弄地呱叫道：「現在你想偷誰的睡眠呀？」

In the evening I will peep into the whispering silence of the bamboo forest,
where fireflies squander their light, and will ask every creature I meet,
" Can anybody tell me where the Sleep-stealer lives? "

Who stole sleep from baby's eyes? I must know.

Shouldn't I give her a good lesson if I could only catch her!

I would raid her nest and see where she hoards all her stolen sleep.

I would plunder it all, and carry it home.

I would bind her two wings securely, set her on the bank of the river, and then
let her play at fishing with a reed among the rushes and water-lilies.

When the marketing is over in the evening, and the village children sit in their
mothers' laps, then the night birds will mockingly din her ears with:

" Whose sleep will you steal now? "

開始

「我是從哪裡來的？您在哪裡撿到我的呢？」孩子問媽媽。

她把孩子抱在胸前，又哭又笑地回答說：

「你曾像我的心願般，藏在我心底，我親愛的寶貝。

你曾藏在我孩童時玩的小土偶裡；我每天早上用泥土捏出的神像，那個我當時捏好了、又捏碎的就是你。

你跟我們家的神明一同被供奉著，在祭拜家神的同時，也祭拜了你。

你一直活在我所有的希望和愛中，活在我的生命和我母親的生命裡。

你已經在主導著我們家永垂不朽的神靈膝上，被撫育了世世代代。

THE BEGINNING

" Where have I come from, where did you pick me up? "
    the baby asked its mother.

She answered half crying, half laughing, and clasping the baby to
    her breast, —

" You were hidden in my heart as its desire, my darling.

You were in the dolls of my childhood's games; and when with
    clay I made the image of my god every morning, I made and
    unmade you then.

You were enshrined with our household deity, in his worship
    I worshipped you.

In all my hopes and my loves, in my life, in the life of my mother
    you have lived.

In the lap of the deathless Spirit who rules our home you have
    been nursed for ages.

當我還是少女，心如花瓣綻開時，你就像花香常伴左右。

你稚嫩的柔軟在我青春肢體上綻放開來，就像日出前，灑現在空中的光芒。

你是天堂裡最受寵、與晨曦一同誕生的孿生兄弟，你隨著世界的生命之流浮游而下，最後終於停在我心頭。

當我凝視著你的臉時，那股神祕感震撼著我；原屬於所有人的你，竟變成了我的。

我因害怕失去你，而將你緊緊抱在懷裡。是什麼魔法將世界的寶貝引領至我細弱的雙臂裡？」

When in girlhood my heart was opening its petals, you hovered as a fragrance about it.

Your tender softness bloomed in my youthful limbs, like a glow in the sky before the sunrise.

Heaven's first darling, twin-born with the morning light, you have floated down the stream of the world's life, and at last you have stranded on my heart.

As I gaze on your face, mystery overwhelms me; you who belong to all have become mine.

For fear of losing you I hold you tight to my breast. What magic has snared the world's treasure in these slender arms of mine? "

孩子的世界

我願自己能在孩子的內心世界占一個安靜的角落。

我知道星辰會和他說話，天空也會俯身到他面前，用那傻傻的雲朵和彩虹來逗弄他。

那些讓人以為不會說話和看似永不會動彈的傢伙，帶著他們的故事、捧著擺滿亮麗玩具的盤子，悄悄爬到他窗前。

但願我能行走於穿越孩子心中的道路上，毫無障礙；

在那裡，使者徒然奔走於沒有歷史的君主王國間；

在那裡，理智將它的律法當作風箏放飛，真理也讓事實擺脫束縛，得獲自由。

08

BABY'S WORLD

I wish I could take a quiet corner
    in the heart of my baby's very own world.

I know it has stars that talk to him, and a sky that
    stoops down to his face to amuse him with its
    silly clouds and rainbows.

Those who make believe to be dumb, and look as
    if they never could move, come creeping to his
    window with their stories and with trays crowded
    with bright toys.

I wish I could travel by the road that crosses baby's
    mind, and out beyond all bounds;

Where messengers run errands for no cause between
    the kingdoms of kings of no history;

Where Reason makes kites of her laws and flies
    them, and Truth sets Fact free from its fetters.

時機與原因

當我拿那些彩色玩具給你時，我的孩子，我這才瞭解雲間、水上為什麼會如此繽紛，為什麼花朵會渲染上色彩——當我拿那些彩色玩具給你時，我的孩子。

當我唱歌讓你歡舞時，我這才真正瞭解葉子上為什麼會響出音律，為什麼浪濤要將它們合唱的樂聲傳送到靜靜聆聽的地心上——當我唱歌讓你歡舞時。

當我將那些糖果放到你貪心的手掌時，我這才瞭解花萼裡為什麼會有蜜液，果實裡為什麼會藏著甜汁——當我將那些糖果放到你貪心的手掌時。

當我親吻你的臉蛋逗你微笑時，我親愛的寶貝，我這才真正明白晨光從天空帶來什麼樣的歡樂，夏日微風為我的身軀帶來什麼樣的歡愉——當我親吻你逗你微笑時。

The Crescent Moon 新月集

09

WHEN AND WHY

When I bring you coloured toys, my child,
  I understand why there is such a play of colours
  on clouds, on water, and why flowers are painted
  in tints — when I give coloured toys to you, my
  child.

When I sing to make you dance, I truly know why
  there is music in leaves, and why waves send their
  chorus of voices to the heart of the listening earth
  — when I sing to make you dance.

When I bring sweet things to your greedy hands,
  I know why there is honey in the cup of the
  flower, and why fruits are secretly filled with sweet
  juice — when I bring sweet things to your greedy
  hands.

When I kiss your face to make you smile, my darling,
  I surely understand what pleasure streams from
  the sky in morning light, and what delight the
  summer breeze brings to my body — when
  I kiss you to make you smile.

責備

你的眼中為何盈滿眼淚，我的孩子？

總是平白無故責備你是多麼可怕的事情呀！

你寫字時手指及小臉沾上了墨水——他們是因為這樣說你髒兮兮的嗎？

喔，呸！要是滿月的臉上沾了墨水，他們也膽敢嫌它髒嗎？

他們吹毛求疵地責備你，我的孩子。他們總是愛在雞蛋裡挑骨頭。

你玩耍的時候扯破了衣裳——他們是因為這樣說你邋遢的嗎？

喔，呸！秋天早晨從它的碎雲中露出微笑，那他們要怎麼怪它呢？

1 0

DEFAMATION

Why are those tears in your eyes, my child?

How horrid of them to be always scolding you
for nothing!

You have stained your fingers and face with ink
while writing — is that why they call you dirty?

O, fie! Would they dare to call the full moon dirty
because it has smudged its face with ink?

For every little trifle they blame you, my child. They
are ready to find fault for nothing.

You tore your clothes while playing — is that why
they call you untidy?

O, fie! What would they call an autumn morning
that smiles through its ragged clouds?

別在意他們對你說的話，我的孩子。

他們列了一長串你的罪行。大家都知道你喜歡糖果——

他們是因為這樣說你貪心的嗎？

喔，呸！我們是如此愛你，他們又要怎麼數落我們這些人呢？

Take no heed of what they say to you, my child.

They make a long list of your misdeeds.
 Everybody knows how you love sweet things
 — is that why they call you greedy?

O, fie! What then would they call us who love
 you?

審判

11

你愛怎麼說他就怎麼說他吧，但是我清楚知道自己孩子的缺點。

我不是因為他好才愛他的，而是因為他是我的小小孩。

如果只是衡量他的優缺點，你怎會知道他有多可愛？

當我需要責罰他時，他尤成為我生命的一部分。

當我讓他流下眼淚時，我的心也跟著他流淚。

只有我自己有權責罰他，因為唯有深愛他的人才能懲罰他。

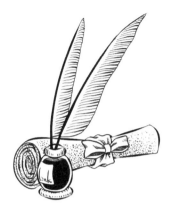

11

THE JUDGE

Say of him what you please,
  but I know my child's failings.

I do not love him because he is good,
  but because he is my little child.

How should you know how dear he can be
  when you try to weigh his merits against
  his faults?

When I must punish him he becomes all
  the more a part of my being.

When I cause his tears to come my heart
  weeps with him.

I alone have a right to blame and punish,
  for he only may chastise who loves.

12 玩具

孩子，你一整個早上坐在泥土上玩著斷枝，該有多快樂呀。

我微笑地看著你玩那小小的斷枝兒。

我正忙著算帳，一個小時又一個小時加總著數字。

或許你會看著我想道：「為什麼要玩這無聊的遊戲，破壞自己美好的早晨！」

孩子，我已經忘記專心玩樹枝與泥巴的方法了。

我追求著昂貴的玩具，收集金塊與銀塊。

無論找到什麼，你總能夠創造出快樂無比的遊戲，而我啊，卻總是將自己的時間與力氣花費在我永遠也得不到的事物上。

我在這艘搖搖欲墜的獨木舟上，掙扎地穿越慾望之海，竟忘了自己也在其中遊戲哩。

12

PLAYTHINGS

Child, how happy you are sitting in the dust, playing
with a broken twig all the morning.

I smile at your play with that little bit of a broken twig.

I am busy with my accounts, adding up figures by
the hour.

Perhaps you glance at me and think, " What a stupid
game to spoil your morning with! "

Child, I have forgotten the art of being absorbed
in sticks and mud-pies.

I seek out costly playthings, and gather lumps of
gold and silver.

With whatever you find you create your glad games,
I spend both my time and my strength over things
I never can obtain.

In my frail canoe I struggle to cross the sea of desire,
and forget that I too am playing a game.

天文學家

我只不過說：「當夜晚滿月纏掛在伽曇波樹的枝頭時，難道沒有人能將它抓下嗎？」

哥哥卻笑著對我說：「小寶貝，你是我見過最傻的孩子了。月亮離我們那麼遠，有誰能抓得到它呢？」

我說：「哥哥你真傻！當媽媽望向窗外，往下笑著看我們玩時，你會說她離我們很遠嗎？」

哥哥還是說：「你真是個傻孩子！但是，小寶貝，你到哪兒去找張大得可以捕住月亮的網呢？」

我說：「雙手就能夠抓住月亮啦。」

1 3

THE ASTRONOMER

I only said, " When in the evening the round full
 moon gets entangled among the branches of that
 Kadam tree, couldn't somebody catch it? "

But dâdâ [elder brother] laughed at me and said,
 " Baby, you are the silliest child I have ever
 known. The moon is ever so far from us, how
 could anybody catch it? "

I said, " Dâdâ, how foolish you are! When mother
 looks out of her window and smiles down at us
 playing, would you call her far away? "

Still dâdâ said, " You are a stupid child! But, baby,
 where could you find a net big enough to catch
 the moon with? "

I said, " Surely you could catch it with your hands. "

The Crescent Moon 新 月 集

可是哥哥笑著說道：「你是我見過最傻的孩子了。等月亮靠近時，你就會曉得月亮有多大了。」

我說：「哥哥，他們在學校可真是教了你一些沒用的東西！當媽媽低下臉來親吻我們時，她的臉看起來也很大嗎？」

但哥哥還是說：「你真是個傻孩子。」

But dâdâ laughed and said, " You are the silliest
child I have known. If it came nearer, you
would see how big the moon is. "

I said, " Dâdâ, what nonsense they teach at your
school! When mother bends her face down to
kiss us does her face look very big? "

But still dâdâ says, " You are a stupid child. "

14 雲與浪

母親，住在雲端上的那些人對我喊道：

「我們從醒來那一刻玩到白晝終了。我們跟金黃色的曙光玩耍、跟銀白色的月亮嬉戲。」

我問道：「可是，我怎麼才能到你們那裡去呢？」

他們回答：「到地球的邊緣，將雙手舉向天，你就會被拉到雲端上了。」

「我媽媽在家等著我呢，」我說，「我怎能離開她來到你們身邊呀？」

他們接著便笑了笑，飄離開了。

但我知道一個比這更好玩的遊戲，母親。

我當雲，您當月亮。

我用雙手遮住您，我們的屋頂就是湛藍的天空。

1 4

CLOUDS AND WAVES

Mother, the folk who live up in the clouds call out to me —

" We play from the time we wake till the day ends. We play with
the golden dawn, we play with the silver moon. "

I ask, " But, how am I to get up to you? "

They answer, " Come to the edge of the earth, lift up your hands
to the sky, and you will be taken up into the clouds. "

" My mother is waiting for me at home, " I say. " How can I
leave her and come? "

Then they smile and float away.

But I know a nicer game than that, mother.

I shall be the cloud and you the moon.

I shall cover you with both my hands, and our house-top will be
the blue sky.

住在波浪上的那些人對我喊道：

「我們從早唱到晚，一直走著路，不知道自己已經過了些什麼地方。」

我問道：「可是，我要怎麼才能到你們那裡去呢？」

他們跟我說：「到海岸邊，緊閉著雙眼站在那裡，波浪就會把你們拉上來了。」

我說：「我的母親總希望我晚上好好待在家裡——我怎能離開她，跟你們走呢？」

他們接著便笑了笑，舞著離開了。

但我知道一個比這更好玩的遊戲。

我當海浪，您當那陌生的海岸。

我會一次又一次滾到岸邊，笑著撞您的膝。

世上沒有人知道我們在哪裡。

The folk who live in the waves call out to me —

" We sing from morning till night; on and on
we travel and know not where we pass. "

I ask, " But, how am I to join you? "

They tell me, " Come to the edge of the shore
and stand with your eyes tight shut, and you
will be carried out upon the waves. "

I say, " My mother always wants me at home in
the evening — how can I leave her and go? "

Then they smile, dance and pass by.

But I know a better game than that.

I will be the waves and you will be a strange
shore.

I shall roll on and on and on, and break upon
your lap with laughter.

And no one in the world will know where we
both are.

金色花

假設我純為了好玩而變成一朵金色花①，長在那高高的枝頭上，笑著隨風搖曳，在新生的葉子上舞動著，您還會認得我嗎，媽媽？

您可能會喊道：「寶貝呀，你在哪裡？」而我會一聲不響地躲在那裡暗自偷笑。

我會悄悄打開花瓣，看著您工作。

當您沐浴完，濕髮還披落在雙肩時，您走過金色花下的林蔭，來到禱告的小庭院，您會聞到花朵香氣，卻不知道那是我散發出來的。

15

THE CHAMPA FLOWER

Supposing I became a *champa* flower, just for fun, and grew
    on a branch high up that tree, and shook in the wind
    with laughter and danced upon the newly budded leaves,
    would you know me, mother?

You would call, " Baby, where are you? " and I should laugh
    to myself and keep quite quiet.

I should slyly open my petals and watch you at your work.

When after your bath, with wet hair spread on your shoulders,
    you walked through the shadow of the *champa* tree to the
    little court where you say your prayers, you would notice
    the scent of the flower, but not know that it came from me.

午飯過後，當您坐在窗前讀著《羅摩衍那》②時，樹影落在您的頭髮與膝上，我會在您的書頁中投下我小小的影子，就剛好落在您正讀到的地方。

但是您會猜得到這是您孩子的小小身影嗎？

◯

到了晚上，當您手拿著燈到牛棚時，我會突然又跳回人間，再度變成了您的寶貝，求您跟我講故事。

「你跑到哪兒去啦，你這淘氣的孩子？」

「我不告訴您，媽媽。」那將會是您和我的對話。

註

① 此處「金色花」的原文為 Champa Flower，為印度聖樹所產之花，木蘭科含笑屬，一般稱「黃玉蘭」，雲南一帶又可叫做「緬桂花」。

② 《羅摩衍那》（Ramayana）是印度兩大史詩之一，另一部為《摩訶婆羅多》（Mahabharata）。

When after the midday meal you sat at the window reading
Ramayana, and the tree's shadow fell over your hair and
your lap, I should fling my wee little shadow on to the
page of your book, just where you were reading.

But would you guess that it was the tiny shadow of your
little child?

When in the evening you went to the cow-shed with the
lighted lamp in your hand, I should suddenly drop on to
the earth again and be your own baby once more, and beg
you to tell me a story.

" Where have you been, you naughty child? "

" I won't tell you, mother. " That's what you and I would say
then.

童話世界

如果讓人們知道了我的國王宮殿在哪裡，宮殿便會消失無蹤。

牆壁是白銀打造的，屋頂則是燦爛的黃金。

皇后住在有七進院落的宮殿裡，穿戴著整整與七個王國等值的珠寶。

但讓我告訴您，母親，讓我偷偷地告訴您我的國王宮殿在哪裡。

它就在我們陽臺上放著聖羅勒盆栽的那個角落。

公主在七海之外那處遙不可及的岸邊沉睡著。

這世界上除了我，再沒有人能找得到她。

1 6

FAIRYLAND

If people came to know where my king's palace is, it would
    vanish into the air.

The walls are of white silver and the roof of shining gold.

The queen lives in a palace with seven courtyards, and she
    wears a jewel that cost all the wealth of seven kingdoms.

But let me tell you, mother, in a whisper, where my king's
    palace is.

It is at the corner of our terrace where the pot of the *tulsi*
    plant stands.

The princess lies sleeping on the far-away shore of the seven
    impassable seas.

There is none in the world who can find her but myself.

她腕上戴著手鐲，耳朵掛著珍珠，秀髮長曳在地。

我拿著魔杖向她一點，她便會醒來；而當她微笑時，珠寶就會從她雙唇落下。

但是母親，讓我在您耳邊偷偷告訴您，她就在我們陽臺上放著聖羅勒盆栽的那個角落。

到了您該去河邊沐浴的時刻，走上屋頂陽臺吧。

我就坐在各面牆影交會的角落。

我只准小貓跟隨我一起來，因為牠知道故事裡的理髮匠住在哪兒。

但是母親，讓我在您耳邊偷偷告訴您，故事裡的理髮匠住在哪兒吧！

就在我們陽臺上放著聖羅勒盆栽的那個角落哦。

She has bracelets on her arms and pearl drops in her ears;
her hair sweeps down upon the floor.

She will wake when I touch her with my magic wand,
and jewels will fall from her lips when she smiles.

But let me whisper in your ear, mother; she is there in
the corner of our terrace where the pot of the *tulsi*
plant stands.

When it is time for you to go to the river for your bath,
step up to that terrace on the roof.

I sit in the corner where the shadows of the walls meet
together.

Only puss is allowed to come with me, for she knows
where the barber in the story lives.

But let me whisper, mother, in your ear where the barber
in the story lives.

It is at the corner of the terrace where the pot of the *tulsi*
plant stands.

流放之地

媽媽，天色變暗了，我不知道現在幾點鐘。

我的遊戲有點無聊了，所以我來找您。今天是週六，我們的休假日。

放下您手邊的工作吧，媽媽，坐到窗邊來，告訴我童話故事裡的特潘塔沙漠在哪裡。

雨的影子遮蓋了整個白天。

可怕的閃電用它的爪子抓住天空。

當烏雲轟隆隆地打起雷時，我喜歡懷著恐懼依偎在您身邊。

當大雨劈哩啪啦在竹葉上打了好幾個小時，窗戶也被狂風震得格格作響時，我喜歡

單獨和您坐在房裡，媽媽，聽您講童話中特潘塔沙漠裡發生的故事。

17

THE LAND OF THE EXILE

Mother, the light has grown grey in the sky; I do not know
what the time is.

There is no fun in my play, so I have come to you. It is Saturday,
our holiday.

Leave off your work, mother; sit here by the window and tell
me where the desert of Tepântar in the fairy tale is?

The shadow of the rains has covered the day from end to end.

The fierce lightning is scratching the sky with its nails.

When the clouds rumble and it thunders, I love to be afraid in
my heart and cling to you.

When the heavy rain patters for hours on the bamboo leaves,
and our windows shake and rattle at the gusts of wind, I like
to sit alone in the room, mother, with you, and hear you talk
about the desert of Tepântar in the fairy tale.

那沙漠到底在哪裡呢，媽媽？在哪座海洋的岸邊，哪座山的腳下，還是哪位國王的王國裡？

那裡沒有籬笆圍界田園，也沒有路讓村民於日落時分穿過田野回村莊，或者讓在林子裡揀拾乾材的婦女運載到市場去。沙地上只有幾塊黃草地及一棵樹，一對聰明的老鳥在樹上頭築了個巢，特潘塔沙漠就在那裡。

我可以想像在這樣烏雲密布的天氣，國王的那個小兒子如何獨自騎著那匹灰馬穿過沙漠，橫越不知名的海域，尋找被囚禁在巨人宮裡的公主。

雨霧於遙遠天際降下，閃電像一陣突如其來的痛楚發作，當他騎過童話故事裡的特潘塔沙漠時，可否想起自己被國王拋棄的不幸母親，正在清掃著牛棚、拭著眼淚？

Where is it, mother, on the shore of what sea, at the foot of what hills, in the kingdom of what king?

There are no hedges there to mark the fields, no footpath across it by which the villagers reach their village in the evening, or the woman who gathers dry sticks in the forest can bring her load to the market. With patches of yellow grass in the sand and only one tree where the pair of wise old birds have their nest, lies the desert of Tepântar.

I can imagine how, on just such a cloudy day, the young son of the king is riding alone on a grey horse through the desert, in search of the princess who lies imprisoned in the giant's palace across that unknown water.

When the haze of the rain comes down in the distant sky, and lightning starts up like a sudden fit of pain, does he remember his unhappy mother, abandoned by the king, sweeping the cow-stall and wiping her eyes, while he rides through the desert of Tepântar in the fairy tale?

看呀，媽媽，白晝還未結束，天色就已經快黑了，村莊的路上沒有什麼人。

牧羊童早早從牧場回家了，人們也已從田裡返回，坐在他們小屋屋簷下的草蓆上，望著陰沉的烏雲。

媽媽，我把所有書都丟在書架上——別要我現在去做功課。

等我長大，大得像爸爸時，我自然便能學會所有該學的了。

但是，媽媽，就今天，趕緊告訴我童話故事裡的特潘塔沙漠在哪裡吧？

See, mother, it is almost dark before the day is over, and
    there are no travellers yonder on the village road.

The shepherd boy has gone home early from the pasture,
    and men have left their fields to sit on mats under the
    eaves of their huts, watching the scowling clouds.

Mother, I have left all my books on the shelf — do not ask
    me to do my lessons now.

When I grow up and am big like my father, I shall learn all
    that must be learnt.

But just for to-day, tell me, mother, where the desert of
    Tepântar in the fairy tale is?

18 雨天

黑壓壓的烏雲快速聚集在森林那黑色邊緣。

喔，孩子，別跑出去！

湖邊那一排棕櫚樹正把頭撞向那一片黑壓壓的天空；雙翅髒亂的烏鴉靜靜地停在羅望樹枝上，漸深的黑沉襲往河的東岸。

我們綁在籬笆旁的牛，大聲地哞叫著。

喔，孩子，在這裡等著，等我把牛牽進牛棚。

人們已經聚集在淹滿水的田間，準備抓從漲溢池塘裡跑出來的魚兒。

雨水匯成涓涓水流，流過狹窄街巷，就像一個笑鬧著的孩子，從母親身邊跑開，故意惹她生氣。

18

THE RAINY DAY

Sullen clouds are gathering fast over the black fringe of the
forest.

O child, do not go out!

The palm trees in a row by the lake are smiting their heads
against the dismal sky; the crows with their draggled wings
are silent on the tamarind branches, and the eastern bank of
the river is haunted by a deepening gloom.

Our cow is lowing loud, tied at the fence.

O child, wait here till I bring her into the stall.

Men have crowded into the flooded field to catch the fishes as
they escape from the overflowing ponds; the rain water is
running in rills through the narrow lanes like a laughing boy
who has run away from his mother to tease her.

聽呀，有人從渡口淺灘呼喊著船夫哩。

喔，孩子，日光漸暗，渡口的擺渡也休止了。

天空好像在瘋狂傾瀉的大雨中奔跑著，河水又大又急，婦女們早就從恆河裝滿水匆匆回家了。

晚上要用的燈，記得先準備好。

喔，孩子，別跑出去！

往市場的路已毫無人煙，往河畔的路很滑。風在竹枝間咆哮、掙扎著，就像一隻被困在網子裡的野獸。

Listen, someone is shouting for the boatman at the ford.

O child, the daylight is dim, and the crossing at the
ferry is closed.

The sky seems to ride fast upon the madly-rushing rain;
the water in the river is loud and impatient; women
have hastened home early from the Ganges with their
filled pitchers.

The evening lamps must be made ready.

O child, do not go out!

The road to the market is desolate, the lane to the river
is slippery. The wind is roaring and struggling among
the bamboo branches like a wild beast
tangled in a net.

19

紙船

我日復一日將我的紙船一只只放入潺潺溪水中。

以大大的黑字書寫上我的名字及我所住村莊之名。

希望在陌生土地上的某個人能發現這些船，還知道我是誰。

我從我們園子裡摘了束秀利花放在我的小船上，希望這批拂曉綻放的花朵，到了夜裡能被安全地帶上岸。

我將我的紙船放到河裡，抬頭仰望天空，看著小小雲朵揚起它們張鼓的白帆。

我不知道自個兒在天上有什麼玩伴，將這些船放下來和我的船比賽！

入夜之後，我將臉埋進臂彎裡，夢見我的紙船在午夜星空下漂流向前。

睡夢仙子坐在這一艘艘船上，帶著裝滿夢的籃子。

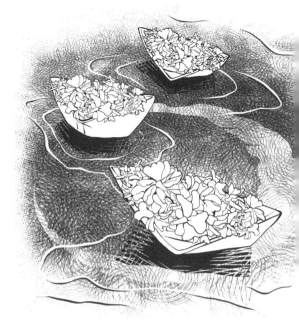

1 9

PAPER BOATS

Day by day I float my paper
boats one by one down the running stream.

In big black letters I write my name on them and the name of
the village where I live.

I hope that someone in some strange land will find them and
know who I am.

I load my little boats with *shiuli* flowers from our garden, and
hope that these blooms of the dawn will be carried safely to
land in the night.

I launch my paper boats and look up into the sky and see the
little clouds setting their white bulging sails.

I know not what playmate of mine in the sky sends them down
the air to race with my boats!

When night comes I bury my face in my arms and dream that
my paper boats float on and on under the midnight stars.

The fairies of sleep are sailing in them, and the lading is their
baskets full of dreams.

水手

船夫馬杜的船停放在拉古尼碼頭。

要是他願意把船借給我，我會為它裝上一百支船槳，揚起五面、六面或七面船帆。

我要航向童話世界裡的七大洋與十三條江河。

然而，媽媽，您別躲在角落為我哭泣。

我不會像羅摩犍陀羅③跑到森林裡，十四年後才回來。

我將變成故事中的王子，船上載滿我喜歡的東西。

船上裝滿一無用處的黃麻，已閒置在那兒好長一段時間了。

我絕不會將這艘船開進愚蠢的市集。

20

THE SAILOR

The boat of the boatman Madhu is moored at the wharf of
Rajgunj.

It is uselessly laden with jute, and has been lying there idle for
ever so long.

If he would only lend me his boat, I should man her with
a hundred oars, and hoist sails, five or six or seven.

I should never steer her to stupid markets.

I should sail the seven seas and the thirteen rivers of fairyland.

But, mother, you won't weep for me in a corner.

I am not going into the forest like Ramachandra to come back
only after fourteen years.

I shall become the prince of the story, and fill my boat with
whatever I like.

我還會帶上我的朋友阿蘇，一起快快樂樂地航行過童話故事裡的七大洋與十三條江河。

我們會在破曉晨曦中揚帆出發。

當您午間在池中沐浴時，我們應該已到了一個陌生的國度。

我們會經過特普尼灘，將特潘塔沙漠拋在我們身後。

當天色漸暗，我們歸來之時，我會告訴您許多我們的所見所聞。

我將航行過童話故事裡的七大洋與十三條江河。

註

③ 即《羅摩衍那》史詩的主角羅摩，亦是主神毗濕奴的眾多化身之一。故事中，羅摩和妻子退居森林十四年，與魔王相抗、奪回妻子後才登上王位。

I shall take my friend Ashu with me. We shall sail merrily
across the seven seas and the thirteen rivers of fairyland.

We shall set sail in the early morning light.

When at noontide you are bathing at the pond, we shall be
in the land of a strange king.

We shall pass the ford of Tirpurni, and leave behind us the
desert of Tepântar.

When we come back it will be getting dark, and I shall tell
you of all that we have seen.

I shall cross the seven seas and the thirteen rivers of
fairyland.

對岸

我渴望到河對岸去。

那裡有一整排船綁在竹竿上；

人們早上划著船過河，肩扛著鋤頭到遠處田地裡耕作；

那裡的牧人趕著哞哞叫的牛涉水游到對岸的牧場；

傍晚時他們全都回家了，只留下豺狼在長滿野草的島上嚎叫著。

母親，如果您不介意，我長大以後想成為這渡口的船夫。

人們說高岸後面藏著些奇怪的池塘。

一群群的野鴨總會在雨後飛到那裡去，池邊長滿了蘆葦，水鳥

會在那兒下蛋；

2 1

THE FURTHER BANK

I long to go over there to the further bank of the river,

Where those boats are tied to the bamboo poles in a line;

Where men cross over in their boats in the morning with
ploughs on their shoulders to till their far-away fields;

Where the cowherds make their lowing cattle swim across to
the riverside pasture;

Whence they all come back home in the evening, leaving the
jackals to howl in the island overgrown with weeds.

Mother, if you don't mind, I should like to become the
boatman of the ferry when I am grown up.

They say there are strange pools hidden behind that high bank,

Where flocks of wild ducks come when the rains are over, and
thick reeds grow round the margins where waterbirds lay
their eggs;

竹雞會搖擺著尾巴，將牠們小小足印留在乾淨的軟泥上；

入夜後，長草頂著白花，邀請月光蕩游在它們的草波間。

母親，如果您不介意，我長大以後想成為這渡口的船夫。

我將往返於兩岸，村裡所有在河中沐浴的男孩與女孩，都驚奇地看著我。

當太陽爬上了半空，清晨變為中午時，我會跑向您喊著：「媽媽，我餓了！」

待一天結束，影子蜷伏在樹下時，我會踏著暮色回家。

我鐵定不會像爸爸那樣離開您到城裡工作。

母親，如果您不介意，我長大以後想成為這渡口的船夫。

Where snipes with their dancing tails stamp their tiny
footprints upon the clean soft mud;

Where in the evening the tall grasses crested with white
flowers invite the moonbeam to float upon their waves.

Mother, if you don't mind, I should like to become the
boatman of the ferryboat when I am grown up.

I shall cross and cross back from bank to bank, and all the
boys and girls of the village will wonder at me while they
are bathing.

When the sun climbs the mid sky and morning wears on to
noon, I shall come running to you, saying, " Mother, I am
hungry! "

When the day is done and the shadows cower under the trees,
I shall come back in the dusk.

I shall never go away from you into the town to work like
father.

Mother, if you don't mind, I should like to become the
boatman of the ferryboat when I am grown up.

花的學校

當雷雲在空中轟轟作響，落下六月陣雨時，

濕潤的東風吹過荒野，在竹林間吹奏它的風笛。

一堆花朵突然不知從哪兒冒了出來，在綠草上狂歡跳舞著。

媽媽，我真的認為那些花朵是在地底學校上學。

它們關上門做功課，如果它們想在放學前跑出來玩，老師

就會要它們在牆角罰站。

22

THE FLOWER-SCHOOL

When storm clouds rumble in the sky and June showers
come down,

The moist east wind comes marching over the heath to blow
its bagpipes among the bamboos.

Then crowds of flowers come out of a sudden, from nobody
knows where, and dance upon the grass in wild glee.

Mother, I really think the flowers go to school underground.

They do their lessons with doors shut, and if they want to
come out to play before it is time, their master makes them
stand in a corner.

一下雨，它們便放假了。

林裡的枝葉交錯在一起，樹葉在狂風中簌簌作響，雷雲拍打著巨大的手，花孩子們即穿上粉紅色、黃色和白色的衣服衝了出來。

您知道麼，母親，它們的家在天空上，在星星住的地方。

您沒看到它們如何急著到那裡去嗎？您難道不知道它們為何如此匆忙嗎？

我當然猜得出來它們是對誰張開手臂的：它們其實就跟我一樣，也有自己的媽媽。

When the rains come they have their holidays.

Branches clash together in the forest, and the leaves rustle in
the wild wind, the thunder-clouds clap their giant hands
and the flower children rush out in dresses of pink and
yellow and white.

Do you know, mother, their home is in the sky, where the stars
are.

Haven't you seen how eager they are to get there? Don't you
know why they are in such a hurry?

Of course, I can guess to whom they raise their arms: they have
their mother as I have my own.

商人

想像一下，媽媽，假設您待在家裡，而我到外地旅行。

想像我的船已經載滿了貨物，準備啟航。

現在，好好想想再告訴我，媽媽，我回來時應該帶什麼東西給您。

媽媽，您想要成堆的黃金嗎？

看呀，在金黃河流的兩岸，田野裡全都是金色穀物。

而林蔭下的林間小徑，金色花落滿地。

我會將之全部拾起，裝在好幾百只籃子裡。

2 3

THE MERCHANT

Imagine, mother, that you are to stay at home and I am to
    travel into strange lands.

Imagine that my boat is ready at the landing fully laden.

Now think well, mother, before you say what I shall bring for
    you when I come back.

Mother, do you want heaps and heaps of gold?

There, by the banks of golden streams, fields are full of golden
    harvest.

And in the shade of the forest path the golden *champa* flowers
    drop on the ground.

I will gather them all for you in many hundred baskets.

媽媽，您想要像秋天雨點般大的珍珠嗎？

我會渡海到珍珠島岸。在那裡，珍珠在清晨曙光中，向草地上的花朵顫動著，珍珠落在草葉間，被狂野的浪濤噴灑在沙灘上。

哥哥呢，應該擁有一對長著翅膀、可以飛上雲端的馬。

而我應該帶枝魔術筆給父親，他想都不用想，字便自己寫了出來。

您呢，媽媽，我一定要拿到那只值上七個王國的珠寶箱送給您。

Mother, do you want pearls big as the raindrops of autumn?

I shall cross to the pearl island shore. There in the early morning light pearls tremble on the meadow flowers, pearls drop on the grass, and pearls are scattered on the sand in spray by the wild sea-waves.

My brother shall have a pair of horses with wings to fly among the clouds.

For father I shall bring a magic pen that, without his knowing, will write of itself.

For you, mother, I must have the casket and jewel that cost seven kings their kingdoms.

同情

如果我只是隻小小狗，不是您的孩子，親愛的媽媽，當我想吃您碟子裡的食物時，您會對我說「不」嗎？

您會不會趕我走，對我說：「走開，你這頑皮的小狗！」

那麼我會走，媽媽，我會走的！您再怎麼叫我，我都不會再到您身邊，也絕不會再要您餵我了。

如果我只是一隻小小的綠色鸚鵡，不是您的寶貝，親愛的媽媽，您會怕我飛走而用鍊子綁著我嗎？

您會不會晃動手指對我說：「真是隻不知感恩的可惡小鳥！每天每夜都啃咬著鍊子。」

那麼我會走，媽媽，我會走的！我會跑到林子裡，永遠不會再讓您將我抱在您的臂彎裡。

24

SYMPATHY

If I were only a little puppy, not your baby, mother dear,
    would you say " No " to me if I tried to eat from your
    dish?

Would you drive me off, saying to me, " Get away, you
    naughty little puppy? "

Then go, mother, go! I will never come to you when you
    call me, and never let you feed me any more.

If I were only a little green parrot, and not your baby,
    mother dear, would you keep me chained lest I
    should fly away?

Would you shake your finger at me and say, " What an
    ungrateful wretch of a bird! It is gnawing at its chain
    day and night? "

Then, go, mother, go! I will run away into the woods;
    I will never let you take me in your arms again.

職業

早晨鐘敲十下時，我沿著我們的小巷走路上學去。

我每天都會遇到一名小販喊著：「手鐲，亮晶晶的手鐲！」

他一點也不趕時間，沒有固定要走的路線，沒有他一定要去的地方，也不一定什麼時間就得趕回到家。

我真希望自己是個小販，整天在街上喊著：「手鐲，亮晶晶的手鐲！」

下午四點，我從學校回來。

從一戶人家的大門，我看到裡面有位園丁在掘著地。

25

VOCATION

When the gong sounds ten in the morning and I walk to school
by our lane,

Every day I meet the hawker crying, " Bangles, crystal bangles! "

There is nothing to hurry him on, there is no road he must take,
no place he must go to, no time when he must come home.

I wish I were a hawker, spending my day in the road, crying,
" Bangles, crystal bangles! "

When at four in the afternoon I come back from the school,
I can see through the gate of that house the gardener digging
the ground.

他拿著鋤頭，愛挖什麼就挖什麼，衣服都被泥土弄髒了。要是他讓太陽曬黑了或被雨淋濕了，也沒人會罵他。

我真希望自己是個園丁，愛怎麼在園裡挖地，都不會有人來阻止我。

晚上天一黑，媽媽就要我上床睡覺。

我從開著的窗口看到巡夜人來回走著。

那條路又暗又寂靜，街燈就像頭上長隻紅眼睛的巨人站在那裡。

巡夜人晃著燈籠，影子隨行在側，他一生從未上床睡過一覺。

我真希望自己是個巡夜人，整晚在街上走著，提著燈籠追著影子跑。

He does what he likes with his spade, he soils his clothes with dust, nobody takes him to task if he gets baked in the sun or gets wet.

I wish I were a gardener digging away at the garden with nobody to stop me from digging.

Just as it gets dark in the evening and my mother sends me to bed,

I can see through my open window the watchman walking up and down.

The lane is dark and lonely, and the street-lamp stands like a giant with one red eye in its head.

The watchman swings his lantern and walks with his shadow at his side, and never once goes to bed in his life.

I wish I were a watchman walking the streets all night, chasing the shadows with my lantern.

長者

媽媽，您的孩子真傻！她可真幼稚！

竟然分不清街燈與星星的差別。

當我們玩著拿石頭當食物的遊戲時，她還真以為那是可以吃的東西，想把石頭放進嘴巴裡。

當我在她面前翻開書，要她學 a、b、c 時，她竟然把書撕破，還莫名其妙地開心胡嚷；您的孩子就是這樣讀書的。

當我生氣地對她搖搖頭，責罵她，並說她頑皮時，她卻哈哈大笑，覺得那很好玩。

26

SUPERIOR

Mother, your baby is silly! She is so absurdly childish!

She does not know the difference between the lights in the streets and the stars.

When we play at eating with pebbles, she thinks they are real food, and tries to put them into her mouth.

When I open a book before her and ask her to learn her a, b, c, she tears the leaves with her hands and roars for joy at nothing; this is your baby's way of doing her lesson.

When I shake my head at her in anger and scold her and call her naughty, she laughs and thinks it great fun.

大家都知道父親不在，但是玩遊戲時，假使我喊道：「爸爸」，

她仍會興奮地四處張望，以為爸爸就在附近。

當我把我們洗衣工用來載衣服的驢子當學生，並且警告她說我是

校長時，她依然莫名其妙地亂叫，喊我哥哥。

您的孩子想抓住月亮。她真好笑呢，還把甘尼許喊成了甘奴許④。

媽媽，您的孩子真傻，她可真幼稚！

註

④ 甘尼許（Ganesh）是普遍常見的印度名字，同時也是象神之名。

Everybody knows that father is away, but if in play
I call aloud " Father, " she looks about her in
excitement and thinks that father is near.

When I hold my class with the donkeys that our
washerman brings to carry away the clothes and
I warn her that I am the schoolmaster, she will
scream for no reason and call me dâdâ.

Your baby wants to catch the moon. She is so
funny; she calls Ganesh Gânush.

Mother, your baby is silly, she is so absurdly
childish!

小大人

我個子小,因為我還是個小孩。等我到了像爸爸的年紀時,個兒就會變大了。

老師過來跟我說:「時候不早了,去把你的板子和書拿過來。」

我會告訴他:「您難道不知道我已經大得像爸爸,不再需要讀書了嗎?」

老師覺得奇怪地說:「他想的話,可以不用讀書,因為他已經長大了。」

我自己穿好衣服,準備到擁擠的市集去。

叔叔趕過來說:「你會走丟的,我的孩子。讓我帶你去吧!」

我會回答:「難道您看不出來麼,叔叔?我已經大得像爸爸了,我得自己走去市集。」

叔叔會說:「是的,他可以去任何他想去的地方,因為他已經長大了。」

THE LITTLE BIG MAN

I am small because I am a little child. I shall be big when I am as old as my father is.

My teacher will come and say, " It is late, bring your slate and your books. "

I shall tell him, " Do you not know I am as big as father? And I must not have lessons any more. "

My master will wonder and say, " He can leave his books if he likes, for he is grown up. "

I shall dress myself and walk to the fair where the crowd is thick.

My uncle will come rushing up to me and say, " You will get lost, my boy; let me carry you. "

I shall answer, " Can't you see, uncle, I am as big as father? I must go to the fair alone. "

Uncle will say, " Yes, he can go wherever he likes, for he is grown up. "

媽媽沐浴回來時看到我拿錢給保姆，因為我已經知道怎麼自己拿鑰匙開錢盒了。

媽媽問說：「你在做什麼，調皮的孩子？」

我會告訴她：「媽媽，難道您不知道，我已經大得像爸爸了，我得拿錢給保姆。」

媽媽會對自己說：「他可以拿錢給他想給的人，因為他已經長大了。」

爸爸十月放假回來時，以為我還是個孩子，而從城裡帶一些小鞋子、小綢衫回來給我。

我會說：「爸爸，把那些給哥哥吧，因為我已經長得跟您一樣大了。」

父親將會在想了一下後說：「他想要的話，可以自己去買衣服，因為他已經長大了。」

Mother will come from her bath when I am giving money to my
nurse, for I shall know how to open the box with my key.

Mother will say, " What are you about, naughty child? "

I shall tell her, " Mother, don't you know, I am as big as father, and
I must give silver to my nurse. "

Mother will say to herself, " He can give money to whom he likes,
for he is grown up. "

In the holiday time in October father will come home and, thinking
that I am still a baby, will bring for me from the town little shoes
and small silken frocks.

I shall say, " Father, give them to my dâdâ, for I am as big as you are. "

Father will think and say, " He can buy his own clothes if he likes, for
he is grown up. "

十二點鐘

媽媽，我現在真的不想做功課，我已經讀了一整個早上的書了。

您說現在才十二點鐘。即使現在還不到十二點鐘，您就不能把十二點想成是下午了嗎？

我輕而易舉便可將這時的太陽想成已經落到稻田邊啦，老漁婦在池塘邊採著晚餐要吃的野菜。

我只要一閉上眼，便能想像得到馬達樹⑤下的影子越來越深暗，池裡的水黑得發亮。

要是十二點鐘能在午夜裡降臨，那麼黑夜為何不能在正午十二點鐘報到呢？

註

⑤孟加拉語為馬達樹（Madar），即中文的「牛角瓜」，別稱「皇冠花」，屬於直立灌木植物。

28

TWELVE O'CLOCK

Mother, I do want to leave off my lessons now. I have been at
my book all the morning.

You say it is only twelve o'clock. Suppose it isn't any later; can't
you ever think it is afternoon when it is only twelve o'clock?

I can easily imagine now that the sun has reached the edge of
that rice-field, and the old fisher-woman is gathering herbs
for her supper by the side of the pond.

I can just shut my eyes and think that the shadows are growing
darker under the *madar* tree, and the water in the pond
looks shiny black.

If twelve o'clock can come in the night, why can't the night
come when it is twelve o'clock?

作者

您說爸爸寫了很多書，但我看不懂他寫的東西。

他整個晚上都在讀給您聽，可是您真的瞭解他寫的東西嗎？

媽媽，您跟我們講的故事多有趣呀！我想不懂，為什麼爸爸就不能寫那樣的故事呢？

莫非他全都忘記了？

難道他從沒聽他媽媽講過巨人、精靈和公主的故事嗎？

他常很晚才沐浴，還得讓您去叫他上百次。

您候著並幫他熱好食物，但他還是繼續埋頭寫作，忘了所有事情。

29

AUTHORSHIP

You say that father writes a lot of books, but what he writes
   I don't understand.

He was reading to you all the evening, but could you really
   make out what he meant?

What nice stories, mother, you can tell us! Why can't father
   write like that, I wonder?

Did he never hear from his own mother stories of giants and
   fairies and princesses?

Has he forgotten them all?

Often when he gets late for his bath you have to go and call
   him an hundred times.

You wait and keep his dishes warm for him, but he goes on
   writing and forgets.

父親總是在玩寫書的遊戲。

要是我到爸爸的房裡玩，您會過來念我：「真是頑皮的孩子！」

要是我發出一丁點聲響，您便會說：「你沒看到父親正在工作嗎？」

老是在寫作到底有什麼好玩的呀？

當我拿起父親的鋼筆或鉛筆，學他在他的書上寫：a、b、c、d、e、f、g、h、i 時，您為什麼會對我發脾氣呢，媽媽？

爸爸寫的時候，您可從未說過一句。

爸爸浪費那麼多紙張，媽媽，您似乎一點也不在意。

但只要我拿一張紙做船時，您就會說：「孩子，你真討厭！」

爸爸在一張又一張的紙兩面都塗滿了黑色記號，您又是怎麼想的呢？

Father always plays at making books.

If ever I go to play in father's room, you come and call me, " What a naughty child! "

If I make the slightest noise, you say, " Don't you see that father's at his work? "

What's the fun of always writing and writing?

When I take up father's pen or pencil and write upon his book just as he does, — a, b, c, d, e, f, g, h, i, — why do you get cross with me, then, mother?

You never say a word when father writes.

When my father wastes such heaps of paper, mother, you don't seem to mind at all.

But if I take only one sheet to make a boat with, you say, " Child, how troublesome you are! "

What do you think of father's spoiling sheets and sheets of paper with black marks all over on both sides?

壞郵差

親愛的媽媽，跟我說說，您為什麼如此安靜沉默地坐在地上？

雨從開著的窗子打進來，您都淋濕了，卻似乎不在意。

您聽到鐘聲敲四下了嗎？該是哥哥放學回家的時候了。

到底發生了什麼事？您的神色看起來好奇怪。

您今天沒收到爸爸的信嗎？

我看見郵差的袋裡裝滿了信，幾乎鎮上每個人都收到信了。

只有爸爸的信，被他留下來自己看了。我可以確定那郵差是個壞人。

30

THE WICKED POSTMAN

Why do you sit there on the floor so quiet and silent, tell me,
   mother dear?

The rain is coming in through the open window, making you
   all wet, and you don't mind it.

Do you hear the gong striking four? It is time for my brother
   to come home from school.

What has happened to you that you look so strange?

Haven't you got a letter from father to-day?

I saw the postman bringing letters in his bag for almost
   everybody in the town.

Only, father's letters he keeps to read himself. I am sure the
   postman is a wicked man.

但別因此而傷心呀，親愛的媽媽。

明天是隔壁村落的市集日，您可以請女傭去幫您買些筆和紙。

我會從 A 一直寫到 K。

但是，媽媽，您為什麼笑了呢？

您不相信我能寫得跟爸爸一樣好嗎？

我會用心寫整齊，把每個字母寫得又大又漂亮。

我寫完之後，您以為我會跟爸爸一樣傻，將信放進那可惡郵差的袋裡嗎？

我會自己馬上將這些信送來給您，並且逐字逐句幫您讀。

我知道那個郵差不願意把真正很棒的信件送來給您。

But don't be unhappy about that, mother dear.

To-morrow is market day in the next village. You ask
your maid to buy some pens and papers.

I myself will write all father's letters; you will not find
a single mistake.

I shall write from A right up to K.

But, mother, why do you smile?

You don't believe that I can write as nicely as father does!

But I shall rule my paper carefully, and write all the letters
beautifully big.

When I finish my writing, do you think I shall be so
foolish as father and drop it into the horrid postman's
bag?

I shall bring it to you myself without waiting, and letter
by letter help you to read my writing.

I know the postman does not like to give you the really
nice letters.

英雄

媽媽，讓我們想像彼此身在旅途上，正通過一個危險的陌生國度。

您坐在一頂轎子裡，而我騎著一匹紅色駿馬跑在您身邊。

那已是晚上，太陽下山了。約拉狄西荒地黯淡無光地在我們面前展開。大地貧脊又荒蕪。

您嚇壞了，在心裡想道：「我真不曉得我們到了什麼地方啦。」

我跟您說：「媽媽，您別害怕。」

草地上長滿帶刺的草，有條崎嶇小徑穿越其間。

在這片浩瀚原野上，看不見任何牛群。牠們全回到村裡的牛棚了。

31

THE HERO

Mother, let us imagine we are travelling, and passing through
    a strange and dangerous country.

You are riding in a palanquin and I am trotting by you on a red
    horse.

It is evening and the sun goes down. The waste of *Joradighi* lies
    wan and grey before us. The land is desolate and barren.

You are frightened and thinking — " I know not where we
    have come to. "

I say to you, " Mother, do not be afraid. "

The meadow is prickly with spiky grass, and through it runs
    a narrow broken path.

There are no cattle to be seen in the wide field; they have gone
    to their village stalls.

天色暗了下來，大地和天空都顯得朦朧昏暗，我們也分不清自己正往哪裡走。

您突然叫了我一聲，低語問道：「河岸邊那是什麼火光呀？」

就在那時，一陣可怕的叫聲突然從那裡發出，幢幢人影朝我們跑來。

您蹲坐在轎子裡，喃喃禱唸著眾神的名字。

轎夫們則嚇得直發抖，躲進荊棘叢裡去了。

我向您喊道：「別害怕，媽媽，有我在這裡。」

他們手持著長木棍，滿頭散髮，越跑越近。

我喊道：「小心啦！你們這些壞蛋！再往前走一步，你們就沒命了。」

他們又發出一陣可怕的叫聲，往前衝了過來。

您抓住我的手，說道：「親愛的孩子，看在上帝的分上，躲開他們吧。」

我回道：「媽媽，您在旁邊看著就好。」

It grows dark and dim on the land and sky, and we cannot tell where we are going.

Suddenly you call me and ask me in a whisper, " What light is that near the bank? "

Just then there bursts out a fearful yell, and figures come running towards us.

You sit crouched in your palanquin and repeat the names of the gods in prayer.

The bearers, shaking in terror, hide themselves in the thorny bush.

I shout to you, " Don't be afraid, mother, I am here. "

With long sticks in their hands and hair all wild about their heads, they come nearer and nearer.

I shout, " Have a care! You villains! One step more and you are dead men. "

They give another terrible yell and rush forward.

You clutch my hand and say, " Dear boy, for heaven's sake, keep away from them. "

I say, " Mother, just you watch me. "

接著我策馬飛奔，劍與盾鏗鏘互相撞擊著。

戰鬥變得如此激烈，媽媽，要是您從轎子裡看得見，肯定嚇得直打冷顫。

他們之中許多人逃走了，也有很多人被砍成碎片。

我知道您自己一個人坐在那裡時，準在心裡想著，您的孩子這次肯定逃不過了。

但我全身濺滿血，跑到您身邊說：「媽媽，戰鬥結束了。」

您走出轎子親吻著我，把我抱在您懷中，自言自語地說：「要是沒有我的孩子保護我，我可真不知道該如何是好了。」

上千件無聊的事情日復一日發生，為什麼這種事不能夠偶爾出現呢？

就像書中的故事。

哥哥會說：「那有可能嗎？我老覺得他弱不禁風的。」

我們村裡的鄉親全要驚訝地說：「還好有那孩子跟他媽媽在一起，真是萬幸，可不是嗎？」

Then I spur my horse for a wild gallop, and my
sword and buckler clash against each other.

The fight becomes so fearful, mother, that it
would give you a cold shudder could you see it
from your palanquin.

Many of them fly, and a great number are cut to
pieces.

I know you are thinking, sitting all by yourself,
that your boy must be dead by this time.

But I come to you all stained with blood, and say,
" Mother, the fight is over now. "

You come out and kiss me, pressing me to your
heart, and you say to yourself, " I don't know
what I should do if I hadn't my boy to escort
me. "

A thousand useless things happen day after day,
and why couldn't such a thing come true by
chance?

It would be like a story in a book.

My brother would say, " Is it possible? I always
thought he was so delicate! "

Our village people would all say in amazement,
" Was it not lucky that the boy was with his
mother? "

告別

該是我離開的時候了，媽媽，我得走了。

在清寂晨幕的灰暗天色裡，您伸了伸手想抱床上的寶貝，我得跟您說：「寶貝不在那兒了！」——媽媽，我得走了。

我會化作一縷輕風，照拂著您；當您沐浴時，我會變成水中的漣漪，一次又一次親吻您。

在風雨不寧的夜晚，當雨滴拍打葉片時，您躺在床上會聽見我的呢喃，我的笑聲也會隨著閃電之光從敞開的窗子照進您房裡。

如果您躺在那兒思念您的孩子，直到半夜還睡不著，我會從星空中哼歌給您聽：「睡吧，媽媽，睡吧。」

3 2

THE END

It is time for me to go, mother; I am going.

When in the paling darkness of the lonely dawn you stretch
out your arms for your baby in the bed, I shall say, " Baby is
not there! " — mother, I am going.

I shall become a delicate draught of air and caress you; and I
shall be ripples in the water when you bathe, and kiss you
and kiss you again.

In the gusty night when the rain patters on the leaves you will
hear my whisper in your bed, and my laughter will flash
with the lightning through the open window into your
room.

If you lie awake, thinking of your baby till late into the night,
I shall sing to you from the stars, " Sleep mother, sleep. "

我會趁您睡著時，隨著游移月光偷偷爬上您的床，躺在您懷裡。

我會變成夢，從您微張眼簾偷溜進您的深眠中；當您醒來，驚訝地看著四周時，我便像閃爍的螢火消失在黑暗中。

而在普耶節⑥這熱鬧節慶，鄰居孩子們來家裡四處跑跳玩鬧著時，我會融入笛子的樂音裡，整日迴盪在您心中。

親愛的阿姨將帶著普耶禮物來，問道：「你的孩子呢，妹妹？」媽媽，您會溫柔地告訴她：「他在我的眼睛裡，在我的身體裡，也在我的靈魂裡。」

The Crescent Moon　新月集

註

⑥普耶節，即是印度十月間的「難近母祭日」。難近母為古婆羅門教中最早崇拜的女神之一，常見形象為三眼十手，騎著獅或虎。

On the straying moonbeams I shall steal over your bed, and lie upon your bosom while you sleep.

I shall become a dream, and through the little opening of your eyelids I shall slip into the depths of your sleep; and when you wake up and look round startled, like a twinkling firefly I shall flit out into the darkness.

When, on the great festival of *puja*, the neighbours' children come and play about the house, I shall melt into the music of the flute and throb in your heart all day.

Dear auntie will come with *puja*-presents and will ask, " Where is our baby, sister? " Mother, you will tell her softly, " He is in the pupils of my eyes, he is in my body and in my soul. "

呼喚

她離去時夜空已經全黑,他們都睡著了。

現在天色依然烏暗,我四處喊著她:「回來吧,親愛的!大地還在沉睡,

當星星互相凝視時,你偷偷來一會兒,沒人會發現的。」

她在樹梢剛萌芽、春天初抵時離去。

現在花朵已經盛開了,我喊著:「回來吧,親愛的!孩子們在漫不經心

的遊戲中,將花撿拾在一起,又把花拋撒開。要是你來拿走一朵小花,沒人

會知道少了一朵的。」

那些只知道玩耍的人,還是一直在玩,如此地虛擲生命。

我聽著那些談話,並喊道:「回來吧,我親愛的!媽媽心中充滿了愛,

你來接受她一個小小的吻,沒有人會嫉妒的。」

33

THE RECALL

The night was dark when she went away, and they slept.

The night is dark now, and I call for her, " Come back, my darling; the world is asleep; and no one would know, if you came for a moment while stars are gazing at stars. "

She went away when the trees were in bud and the spring was young.

Now the flowers are in high bloom and I call, " Come back, my darling. The children gather and scatter flowers in reckless sport. And if you come and take one little blossom no one will miss it. "

Those that used to play are playing still, so spendthrift is life.

I listen to their chatter and call, " Come back, my darling, for mother's heart is full to the brim with love, and if you come to snatch only one little kiss from her no one will grudge it. "

最初的茉莉

啊，這些茉莉花，這些白色的茉莉花！

我似猶記得自己第一次滿手捧著這些茉莉花的模樣，這些白色的茉莉花。

我愛著陽光、天空及綠色大地；

我在午夜的黑暗中，聽到潺潺流水聲；

秋天落日在荒寂的彎路上灑落我身，就像一名掀起頭紗接受愛人的新娘。

然而我仍甜蜜地記得小時候第一次滿手捧著白色茉莉花的模樣。

我生命中曾有過許多快活時光，曾在節慶夜晚隨著製造歡笑的人笑過。

在煙雨濛濛的清晨，我吟唱過許多浪漫詩歌。

我宴會晚裝的脖頸上也曾戴過愛人的手編花環。

然而我仍甜蜜地記得小時候第一次滿手捧著白色茉莉花的模樣。

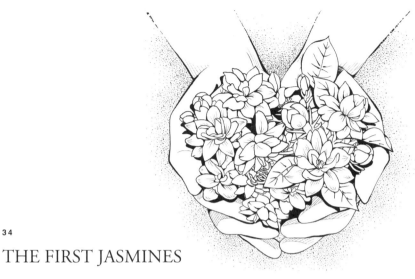

34

THE FIRST JASMINES

Ah, these jasmines, these white jasmines!

I seem to remember the first day when I filled
my hands with these jasmines, these white jasmines.

I have loved the sunlight, the sky and the green earth;

I have heard the liquid murmur of the river through the
darkness of midnight;

Autumn sunsets have come to me at the bend of a road in the
lonely waste, like a bride raising her veil to accept her lover.

Yet my memory is still sweet with the first white jasmines that
I held in my hand when I was a child.

Many a glad day has come in my life, and I have laughed with
merrymakers on festival nights.

On grey mornings of rain I have crooned many an idle song.

I have worn round my neck the evening wreath of *bakulas*
woven by the hand of love.

Yet my heart is sweet with the memory of the first fresh
jasmines that filled my hands when I was a child.

榕樹

喔！你這棵頂著滿頭亂髮站在池邊的榕樹，是否已經忘了那個跟鳥兒一樣在你枝頭上築巢又離開了你的小孩？

難道你不記得他是怎麼坐在窗邊，想著你糾纏的根到底是怎樣扎進地下的？

婦人會帶著她們的水罐到池邊裝水，而你大大的黑影在水中晃動著，就像在睡夢中掙扎著要起來似的。

陽光在水波上漫舞，好似不眠不休的梭機，織著金黃色毯子。

兩隻鴨子於蘆葦邊倒影上游著，而那個小孩仍靜靜地坐在那裡思考。

他渴望成為風，吹過你搖曳的樹枝；想成為你的影子，隨著日光增長；想成為鳥兒，棲息在你最頂端的樹枝上；還想像那兩隻鴨子在蘆葦與倒影間穿梭。

3 5

THE BANYAN TREE

O you shaggy-headed banyan tree standing on the bank of the
  pond, have you forgotten the little child, like the birds that have
  nested in your branches and left you?

Do you not remember how he sat at the window and wondered
  at the tangle of your roots that plunged underground?

The women would come to fill their jars in the pond, and your
  huge black shadow would wriggle on the water like sleep
  struggling to wake up.

Sunlight danced on the ripples like restless tiny shuttles weaving
  golden tapestry.

Two ducks swam by the weedy margin above their shadows,
  and the child would sit still and think.

He longed to be the wind and blow through your rustling
  branches, to be your shadow and lengthen with the day on the
  water, to be a bird and perch on your topmost twig,
  and to float like those ducks among the weeds and shadows.

祝福

36

祝福這小小的心靈，這潔白的靈魂，已經為我們的大地贏得了天堂之吻。

他喜愛陽光，喜愛見到媽媽的臉龐。

他並沒有學到厭惡塵土、渴求黃金。

將他緊緊擁在懷裡，好好祝福他。

他來到這滿是歧路的土地。

我不知道他是如何從人群中選中你，進而來到你家門口，抓著你的手請求指引的。

他跟隨你，笑笑又說說，心底不存半點懷疑。

莫辜負他的信任，帶領他走向正道，好好祝福他。

將你的手貼放在他頭上祈禱，即使波濤底下漸趨險峻，風仍有可能從天而降，鼓起他的船帆，將他推往平和的避風港。

別在忙碌中將他遺忘，讓他來到你心房，好好祝福他。

The Crescent Moon 新月集

BENEDICTION

Bless this little heart, this white soul that has won the kiss of heaven for our earth.

He loves the light of the sun, he loves the sight of his mother's face.

He has not learned to despise the dust, and to hanker after gold.

Clasp him to your heart and bless him.

He has come into this land of an hundred cross-roads.

I know not how he chose you from the crowd, came to your door, and grasped your hand to ask his way.

He will follow you, laughing and talking, and not a doubt in his heart.

Keep his trust, lead him straight and bless him.

Lay your hand on his head, and pray that though the waves underneath grow threatening, yet the breath from above may come and fill his sails and waft him to the haven of peace.

Forget him not in your hurry, let him come to your heart and bless him.

禮物

我想給你點東西，我的孩子，因我們都漂流在世界之河中。

我們的生命將分道揚鑣，愛也會被遺忘。

但我並沒有傻到希冀拿禮物來收買你的心。

你的生命正青春，路還長著，你一口氣飲盡我們給你的愛，接著便轉身從我們身邊跑開了。

你有自己的玩樂及玩伴，沒時間或沒心思想到我們，這又有什麼傷害呢？

而我們呢，年老時確實有的是時間去細數過往的日子，將從我們手中永遠失去的事物珍藏在心裡。

河流唱著歌匆匆流去，沖破所有屏障。但是青山猶在，記念著種種，並以其不朽之愛相隨。

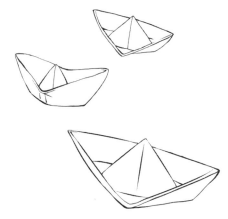

37

THE GIFT

I want to give you something, my child, for we are drifting in
the stream of the world.

Our lives will be carried apart, and our love forgotten.

But I am not so foolish as to hope that I could buy your heart
with my gifts.

Young is your life, your path long, and you drink the love we
bring you at one draught and turn and run away from us.

You have your play and your playmates. What harm is there
if you have no time or thought for us.

We, indeed, have leisure enough in old age to count the days
that are past, to cherish in our hearts what our hands have
lost for ever.

The river runs swift with a song, breaking through all barriers.
But the mountain stays and remembers, and follows her
with his love.

我的歌

我的這首歌會揚起樂音環繞著你，我的孩子，好似愛的柔情臂彎。

我的這首歌將吻觸你的額頭，宛如祝福之吻。

當你獨處時，它會陪伴在你身邊，於你耳畔微語；當你在擁擠的人群時，

它會讓你超然世外，守護著你。

我的歌將化為你夢中的雙翼，將你的心帶往未知的岸邊。

當黑夜覆沒你的道路時，它會像一顆忠心的星辰照在你前頭。

我的歌會駐進你的瞳孔裡，將你的視線帶往事物的中心。

當我的聲音因死亡而靜寂時，我的歌會在你鮮活的心中唱說著。

MY SONG

This song of mine will wind its music around you, my child, like the fond arms of love.

This song of mine will touch your forehead like a kiss of blessing.

When you are alone it will sit by your side and whisper in your ear, when you are in the crowd it will fence you about with aloofness.

My song will be like a pair of wings to your dreams, it will transport your heart to the verge of the unknown.

It will be like the faithful star overhead when dark night is over your road.

My song will sit in the pupils of your eyes, and will carry your sight into the heart of things.

And when my voice is silent in death, my song will speak in your living heart.

孩子天使

他們喧鬧爭吵著，他們失望猜疑，知道他們的爭辯永遠也沒個終了。

讓你的生命進到他們之間去，我的孩子，宛若安定又純潔的光明之火，讓他們歡樂得沉靜下來。

他們在貪婪與嫉妒中是殘暴的，他們的話語宛如隱藏的刀刃，渴欲飲血。

去站在他們憤恨不平的心中，我的孩子，以你溫柔眼眸看向他們，猶如夜晚寬容的和平，蓋過白日的紛擾。

讓他們看看你的臉，我的孩子，讓他們因此瞭解所有事物的真義；讓他們愛你，進而使他們彼此互愛。

來到無垠的懷抱中坐下吧，我的孩子。當旭日初升，讓你的心亦如盛開花朵般打開來，待日落時低下你的頭，在沉默中完成這一天的禱告。

39

THE CHILD-ANGEL

They clamour and fight, they doubt and despair, they know no
end to their wranglings.

Let your life come amongst them like a flame of light, my child,
unflickering and pure, and delight them into silence.

They are cruel in their greed and their envy, their words are like
hidden knives thirsting for blood.

Go and stand amidst their scowling hearts, my child, and let
your gentle eyes fall upon them like the forgiving peace of
the evening over the strife of the day.

Let them see your face, my child, and thus know the meaning
of all things; let them love you and thus love each other.

Come and take your seat in the bosom of the limitless, my child.
At sunrise open and raise your heart like a blossoming flower,
and at sunset bend your head and in silence complete the
worship of the day.

最後的買賣

「來雇用我吧!」當我早晨在鋪石路上走著時,我這麼喊道。

國王駕著他的戰車,手持著劍走來。

他拉起我的手說:「我以我的權力雇用你。」

但是他的權力毫無用處,他登上他的戰車離開了。

日正當中時,家家戶戶都緊閉門戶。

我獨自在某條蜿蜒小巷走著。

有位老人拿著一袋金子走出來。

他想了一下,說道:「我用我的錢雇用你。」

他逐一數著他的金幣,我卻轉身離開。

40

THE LAST BARGAIN

" Come and hire me, " I cried, while in the morning I was
 walking on the stone-paved road.

Sword in hand, the King came in his chariot.

He held my hand and said, " I will hire you with my power. "

But his power counted for nought, and he went away in his
 chariot.

In the heat of the midday the houses stood with shut doors.

I wandered along the crooked lane.

An old man came out with his bag of gold.

He pondered and said, " I will hire you with my money. "

He weighed his coins one by one, but I turned away.

將近黃昏，園子的籬笆開滿了花。

一名美女走出來，對我說：「我以我的微笑雇用你。」

她的微笑黯淡下來化成了淚珠，又獨自走回黑暗中。

太陽在沙地上閃耀著，海浪恣意濺灑開來。

有個孩子坐在那裡玩著貝殼。

他抬起頭來，似乎認識我，開口說：「我兩手空空雇用你。」

從那時起，在這孩童遊戲中做成的買賣，令我成了自由人。

It was evening. The garden hedge was all aflower.

The fair maid came out and said, " I will hire you with a smile. "

Her smile paled and melted into tears, and she went back alone into the dark.

The sun glistened on the sand, and the sea waves broke waywardly.

A child sat playing with shells.

He raised his head and seemed to know me, and said, " I hire you with nothing. "

From thenceforward that bargain struck in child's play made me a free man.

國家圖書館出版品預行編目資料

新月集 / 泰戈爾 (Rabindranath Tagore) 著；伍晴文譯.
-- 二版 . -- 臺中市：好讀出版有限公司 , 2022.10
面： 公分，——（典藏經典；65）
全新插畫雙語版
譯自：The crescent moon.
ISBN 978-986-178-616-2（平裝）

867.51   111012751

好讀出版

典藏經典 65

新月集【全新插畫雙語版】

作　　者／泰戈爾 Rabindranath Tagore
譯　　者／伍晴文
內頁插圖／許承菱
總 編 輯／鄧茵茵
文字編輯／林泳誼、林碧瑩
美術編輯／鄧語萼
行銷企畫／劉恩綺
發行所／好讀出版有限公司
　　　　407 台中市西屯區工業 30 路 1 號
　　　　407 台中市西屯區大有街 13 號（編輯部）
TEL:04-23157795　FAX:04-23144188
http://howdo.morningstar.com.tw
（如對本書編輯或內容有意見，請來電或上網告訴我們）
法律顧問／陳思成律師

讀者服務專線：(02)23672044 / (04)23595819#230
讀者傳眞專線：(02)23635741 / (04)23595493
讀者專用信箱：service@morningstar.com.tw
晨星網路書店：http://www.morningstar.com.tw
郵政劃撥：15062393（知己圖書股份有限公司）
如需詳細出版書目、訂書，歡迎洽詢

二版／西元 2022 年 10 月 15 日
初版／西元 2012 年 9 月 15 日
定價：200 元
如有破損或裝訂錯誤，請寄回知己圖書更換

填寫線上讀者回函
獲得更多好讀資訊